I am a UNICORN!

story and pictures by michaela schuett

Sky Pony Press
New York

Sky Pony Press books may be purchased in bulk at special discounts for sales promotion, corporate gifts, fund-raising, or educational purposes. Special editions can also be created to specifications. For details, contact the Special Sales Department, Sky Pony Press, 307 West 36th Street, 11th Floor, New York, NY 10018 or info@ skyhorsepublishing.com.

Sky Pony® is a registered trademark of Skyhorse Publishing, Inc.®, a Delaware corporation.

Visit our website at www.skyponypress.com.

10 9 8 7 6 5 4 3 2

Manufactured in China, February 2017
This product conforms to CPSIA 2008

Library of Congress Cataloging-in-Publication Data is available on file.

Cover design and illustration by Michaela Schuett

Print ISBN: 978-1-5107-1469-4
Ebook ISBN: 978-1-5107-1470-0

"For Henry and Luella: Always believe in yourselves and the magic you create."

"Nope, you're not."

"Didn't you see my pretty horn?"

"Yes, Frog. I see that.
But you are not a unicorn."

"But I live on a fluffy cloud!

I spread happiness and cheer wherever I go!

My best friend is a fairy!

I eat flowers and
toot rainbows!"

NO, FROG!

You do not live on a fluffy cloud! You cannot fly.

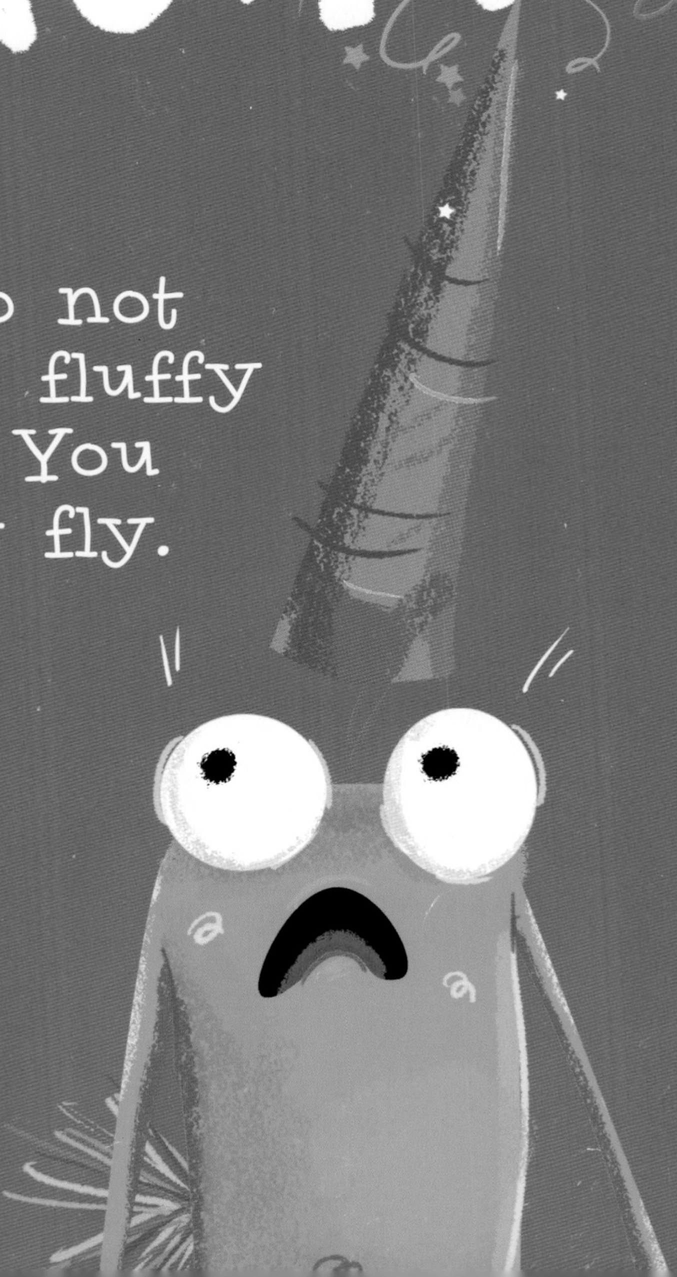

Cow is not a fairy!

You do not eat flowers or toot rainbows.

You do not have magical unicorn sprinkles.

And that is not a UNICORN HORN on your head!

"Good."

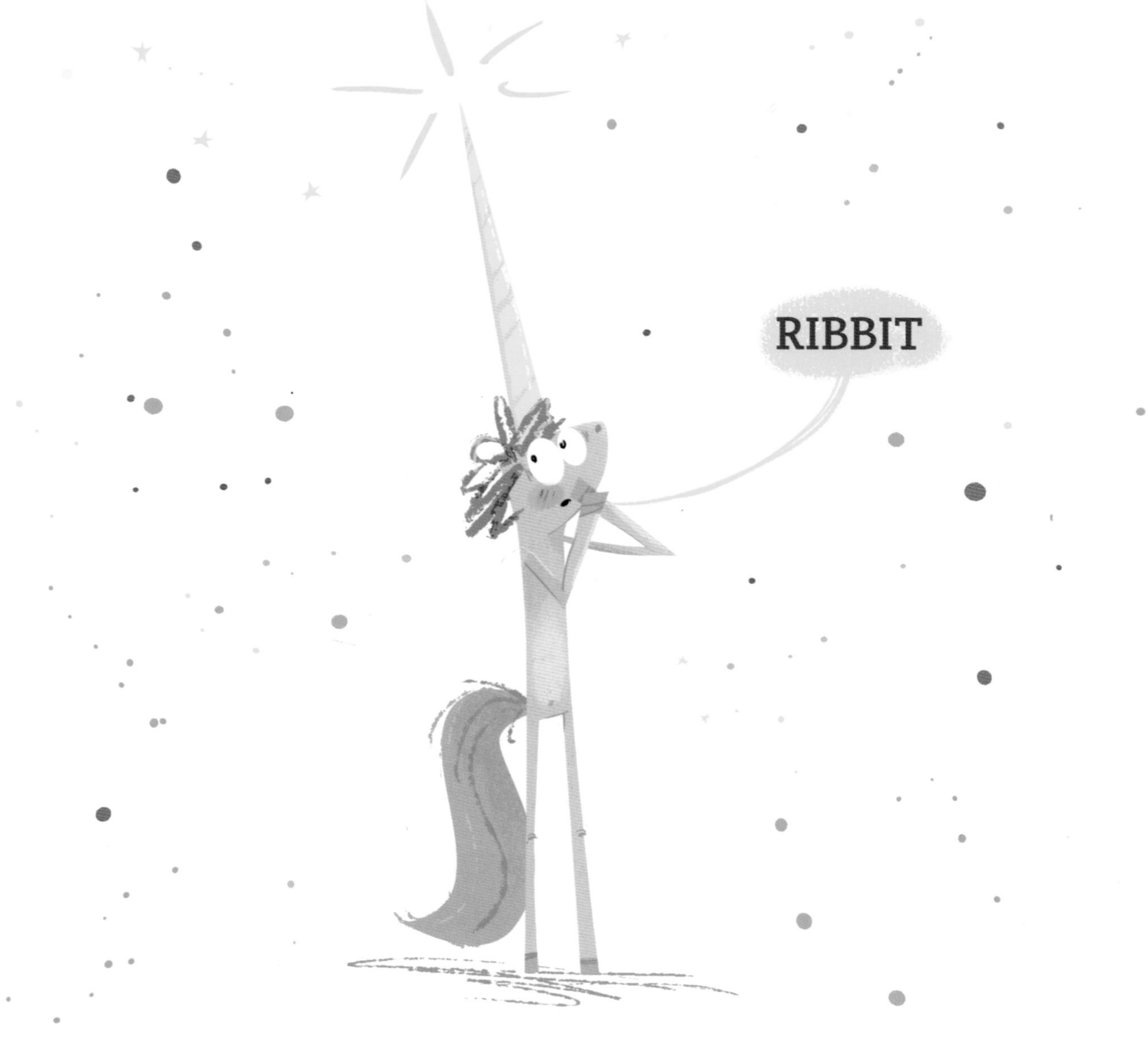
RIBBIT